I AM READI

MR COOL

JACQUELINE WILSON
Illustrated by
STEPHEN LEWIS

MACMILLAN CHILDREN'S BOOKS

First published by Kingfisher 1996

This edition published 2013 by Macmillan Children's Books
a division of Macmillan Publishers Limited
20 New Wharf Road, London N1 9RR
Basingstoke and Oxford
Associated companies throughout the world
www.panmacmillan.com

ISBN 978-1-4472-4723-4

1 3 5 7 9 8 6 4 2

A CIP catalogue record for this book is available from the British Library.

Printed in China

Contents

Chapter One

Ricky wanted to be a rock star.

He was brilliant at singing.

He was brilliant at dancing.

He looked brilliant too.

Ricky had floppy fair hair

that fell into his blue eyes.

Ricky always wore blue denim.

Ricky looked cool.

Micky wanted to be a rock star.

He was terrific at singing.

He was terrific at dancing.

He looked terrific too.

Micky had long red hair

and wicked green eyes.

Micky always wore black.

Micky looked cool.

Nicky wanted to be a rock star.

He was fantastic at singing.

He was fantastic at dancing.

He looked fantastic too.

Nicky had curly black hair

and big brown eyes.

Nicky always wore leather.

Nicky looked cool.

Kevin wanted to be a rock star.

He wasn't great at singing.

He wasn't great at dancing.

He didn't look great either.

Kevin had straight mousey hair
and grey eyes.

Kevin always wore a jumper,
knitted by his nan, and tracksuit bottoms.

Kevin didn't look cool.

But he had a great smile.

Ricky and Micky and Nicky
formed a band.

"Can I be in the band too?"
asked Kevin.

Ricky and Micky and Nicky
weren't sure.

"You're a nice guy, Kevin.

But you're not that great at singing,"
said Ricky.

Kevin smiled bravely.

Ricky felt bad.

"We do like you, Kevin.

But you're not that great at dancing,"
said Micky.

Kevin smiled bravely.

Micky felt bad.

"You can't help it, Kevin.
You just don't look cool,"
said Nicky.
Kevin smiled bravely.
Nicky felt bad.

9

"I wish I could be in your band,"

said Kevin, still smiling.

"Go on, you guys.

Let me be in the band.

I'll try hard at singing.

I'll try hard at dancing.

I'll try hard to look cool."

Ricky and Micky and Nicky

still weren't sure.

"My nan's got a basement," said Kevin.

"We could practise there.

My nan won't mind a bit."

Ricky and Micky and Nicky

didn't have a good place to practise.

11

Ricky lived in a bungalow.
Ricky's mum and dad
moaned and groaned
when the boys in the band
started playing.

12

Micky lived in a house with a lot of pets.
All the pets howled and yowled
when the boys in the band
started playing.

Nicky lived in a flat.

Nicky's neighbours came to his door

and huffed and puffed

when the boys in the band

started playing.

"Could we practise in your nan's basement any time?" Ricky asked Kevin.

"You bet," said Kevin.

"Right," said Ricky.

"You can be in the band then, Kevin. OK, Micky?"

"OK with me," said Micky. "OK, Nicky?"

"OK with me," said Nicky.

"Count yourself
one of the band, Kevin,"
said Ricky.

"G-r-e-a-t!" said Kevin,
and he smiled and smiled and smiled.

Chapter Two

Ricky and Micky and Nicky and Kevin

practised every night

in Kevin's nan's basement.

Kevin's nan brought them drinks

and chocolate biscuits.

The band practised
and practised
and practised.
Ricky and Micky and Nicky
got even better at singing.
Kevin still wasn't that great at singing.

Ricky and Micky and Nicky
got even better at dancing.
Kevin still wasn't that great at dancing.

Ricky and Micky and Nicky
all looked super cool.
Kevin didn't look cool at all.
But Ricky and Micky and Nicky
didn't want to push Kevin
out of the band.

They liked Kevin.

And they needed to practise

in Kevin's nan's basement.

It was Kevin's nan

who got the boys their first gig.

"My friend goes to this club.

They want a band for Saturday night.

I said I know a very good band.

OK with you, boys?" said Kevin's nan.

"OK with me!" said Ricky.

"OK with me!" said Micky.

"OK with me!" said Nicky.

"G-r-e-a-t!" said Kevin.

"Thanks, Nan!"

The band practised even harder
for their Saturday night gig.

"What shall we call our band?"

said Ricky.

"How about Ricky and Micky

and Nicky and Kevin?"

said Kevin.

"That doesn't sound very cool, Kevin,"

said Ricky.

"I'm not a very cool guy,"

said Kevin.

"Not like you, Ricky.

You're a real Mr Cool.

And you, Micky.

You're a real Mr Cool, too.

And you, Nicky.

Yet another

Mr Cool."

"Mr Cool," said Ricky.

He snapped his fingers.

"Brilliant name!"

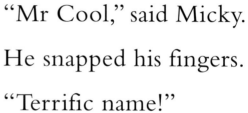

"Mr Cool," said Micky.

He snapped his fingers.

"Terrific name!"

"Mr Cool," said Nicky.

He snapped his fingers.

"Fantastic name!"

"Mr Cool," said Kevin.
He tried to snap his fingers
but they got stuck.
It didn't matter.
"G–r–e–a–t,"
said Kevin,
and he smiled
and smiled
and smiled.

So the boys called the band Mr Cool.

They didn't feel very cool

just before their first gig.

Ricky had problems with his voice.

Micky had problems with his feet.

Nicky had problems with his hair.

Kevin had lots and lots
and lots of problems.
"We're rubbish,"
said Ricky, Micky and Nicky.
"We can't go on."
"I'm rubbish," said Kevin.
"But you guys are
brilliant,
terrific,
fantastic.
We're going to go on.
And we're going
to be great."

So Mr Cool played their first gig.

They were great.

Ricky and Micky and Nicky
were brilliant at singing.

Ricky and Micky and Nicky
were terrific at dancing.

Ricky and Micky and Nicky
looked fantastic.

Kevin still wasn't great at singing.

Or dancing.

Kevin still didn't look great either.

But he had a great smile.

And all the people in the club smiled too.

They clapped and cheered

when the band took a bow.

Mr Cool was a big success.

Chapter Three

Ricky and Micky and Nicky and Kevin

played at the club every Saturday night.

They were asked to play

at lots of other clubs too.

And colleges.

And bars.

They even did a gig at a birthday party,

but that was just for Kevin's nan.

Then one night a man called Mr Rich
came to hear the boys play.
Mr Rich was well known
in the music world.

The boys were very nervous

when they spotted Mr Rich.

"Don't worry, guys," said Kevin.

"We'll be great."

Kevin smiled

and Ricky and Micky and Nicky

smiled back.

 They did their act in front of Mr Rich.

Ricky and Micky and Nicky

were brilliant at singing.

Ricky and Micky and Nicky

were terrific at dancing.

Ricky and Micky and Nicky

looked fantastic too.

Kevin wasn't great at singing.

Kevin wasn't great at dancing.

Kevin didn't look great either,

in spite of his new knitted jumper.

"You boys are incredible," said Mr Rich.

"You're a great band.

I want to sign you up.

Well....I want three of you."

He pointed at Ricky.

He pointed at Micky.

He pointed at Nicky.

He didn't point at Kevin.

He shook his head.

"Sorry, lad," said Mr Rich to Kevin.

"I don't want you in the band."

Kevin stopped smiling.

He nodded sadly and walked away.

"Hang on, Kevin!" said Ricky.

"You're part of Mr Cool.

I say you take all four of us, Mr Rich

– or none of us.

OK with you, boys?"

"OK with me!" said Micky.

"OK with me!" said Nicky.

Kevin didn't say anything.

But he smiled.

"OK with me too,"

said Mr Rich, sighing.

Mr Rich groomed the boys for stardom.

They made their first album.

Ricky and Micky and Nicky

were brilliant at singing

on their first Mr Cool album.

Kevin wasn't that great.

He sang very softly.

They made their first video.

Ricky and Micky and Nicky

were terrific at dancing

on their first Mr Cool video.

Kevin wasn't that great.

He danced out of camera shot

a lot of the time.

They posed for their first

Mr Cool photo shoot.

Ricky and Micky and Nicky

looked fantastic,

really super cool.

Kevin didn't look great.

He stood behind the other boys.

Mr Rich set up a big concert tour

for Mr Cool.

Ricky and Micky and Nicky

were *so* nervous.

Even Mr Rich was a little bit nervous.

But Kevin told them not to worry.

"Stay cool, you guys," he said.

"They'll think we're great, you'll see."

All the girls and boys did think
Mr Cool was a great band.
They thought they were
brilliant, terrific, fantastic.
Ricky and Micky
and Nicky and Kevin sang.
Ricky and Micky and Nicky
and Kevin danced.
Ricky and Micky
and Nicky and Kevin posed
in their new stage outfits.
Kevin chatted
to the audience.
"Hope you're having
a great time," he said,
and he smiled.

He saw his nan at the back.

He waved.

Nan waved back.

And all the girls and boys waved too.

"We're having a great time, Kevin,"
they yelled.

"We love Mr Cool.

We love Ricky.

We love Micky.

We love Nicky.

And most of all – we love you, Kevin!

We think you're g-r-e-a-t!"

Kevin smiled and smiled and smiled.

About the Author and Illustrator

Jacqueline Wilson has written lots of books for children, including *Double Act*, which won the Smarties Book Prize. Jacqueline says, "Kevin certainly doesn't look cool like the rest of the boys in the band – but he's so funny and friendly it doesn't matter a bit."

Stephen Lewis graduated from Art School in 1994 and has been illustrating children's books ever since. "I went to school with lads who formed a band," says Stephen. "They became just as successful as Mr Cool – but none of them was quite like Kevin."

Tips for Beginner Readers

1. Think about the cover and the title of the book. What do you think it will be about? While you are reading, think about what might happen next and why.

2. As you read, ask yourself if what you're reading makes sense. If it doesn't, try rereading or look at the pictures for clues.

3. If there is a word that you do not know, look carefully at the letters, sounds, and word parts that you do know. Blend the sounds to read the word. Is this a word you know? Does it make sense in the sentence?

4. Think about the characters, where the story takes place, and the problems the characters in the story faced. What are the important ideas in the beginning, middle and end of the story?

5. Ask yourself questions like:
Did you like the story?
Why or why not?
How did the author make it fun to read?
How well did you understand it?

Maybe you can understand the story better if you read it again!